Hugo
at the Park

Anne Rockwell

Macmillan Publishing Company   New York
Collier Macmillan Publishers   London

For Nicholas Harlow

10 9 8 7 6 5 4 3 2 1

The text of this book is set in 20 point ITC Newtext Book. The illustrations are rendered in pen and ink and watercolor on paper.

Library of Congress Cataloging-in-Publication Data   Rockwell, Anne F.   Hugo at the park/Anne Rockwell.—1st American ed.   p.   cm. Summary: Hugo the Labrador puppy goes for a walk in the park with his human friend and sees many interesting things.
ISBN 0-02-777301-9
[1. Dogs—Fiction. 2. Parks—Fiction.] I. Title. PZ7.R5943Hv 1990   [E]—dc19
89-2417 CIP AC

It was a beautiful spring day.
Hugo's friend said,

"Let's go to the park!"

"Rrrufff!" said Hugo.

That meant, "Yes, let's go!"

Hugo liked the park.

He liked his new leash.

Hugo saw some people
having a picnic lunch.

Hugo wanted to have
a picnic lunch, too.

"No, no, Hugo!" said his friend.
The picnic lunch
looked good to Hugo,
but he wanted
to make his friend happy.
So he did not eat it.
He and his friend walked on.

They heard a lady singing loudly
while she skated down the path.
Hugo began to sing, too.

He sang very loudly.
People laughed when they heard
Hugo singing with the lady.

"That's enough, Hugo!"
said his friend.
Hugo liked
singing with the lady,
but he wanted
to make his friend happy.
So he stopped.

Lots of people came running by.

Hugo started to run, too.

"Hugo, come! Hugo, sit!"
called Hugo's friend.
Hugo stopped running
with all the people.
He came back to his friend
and he sat.
"What a good boy you are, Hugo,"
said his friend.

Then Hugo and his friend
walked on through the park.
They came to the big pond.

Little toy boats were sailing.
Big white swans were swimming
with the bright goldfish.

"Aaruff-ruff!" said Hugo
to a big white swan.
That was how Hugo said hello.

But that big white swan said,
"Hissssss! Hissssss!"
and flapped its big white wings
at Hugo and his friend.

Hugo did not like that.
He knew that the big white swan
was not saying hello.
"Bow-wow-wow!" said Hugo,
and jumped into the pond.

Hugo made such a loud splash
that he did not hear his friend
calling, "Hugo! Come back!"

Hugo swam fast,
but the big white swan
swam faster.
Hugo swam so fast and so far
that he pulled his friend
into the pond, too.

When Hugo saw his friend
in the water,
he swam back to him.
They climbed out of the pond together.

"Look at us," said Hugo's friend.
"I am all wet and you are, too."

Hugo shook himself dry
and made his friend even wetter.
"Oh, no!" said his friend.

Then Hugo's friend began to laugh.
They stretched out
on the green, green grass.
The warm spring sunshine
began to dry them off.
"Hugo," said his friend,
"even though you got me all wet today,
I love you just the same."
"Woof!" said Hugo softly,
and that meant,
"I love you, too."

Then Hugo went to sleep
on the green grass in the park.